For Mom and Dad —T. T.
For Colleen —J. H.

STERLING CHILDREN'S BOOKS
New York

An Imprint of Sterling Publishing Co., Inc.
1166 Avenue of the Americas
New York, NY 10036

STERLING CHILDREN'S BOOKS and the distinctive
Sterling Children's Books logo are registered trademarks of
Sterling Publishing Co., Inc.

Text © 2018 Todd Tarpley
Cover and interior illustrations © 2018 Jennifer Harney

ISBN 978-1-4549-2330-5

Distributed in Canada by Sterling Publishing Co., Inc.
c/o Canadian Manda Group, 664 Annette Street
Toronto, Ontario M6S 2C8, Canada
Distributed in the United Kingdom by GMC Distribution Services
Castle Place, 166 High Street, Lewes, East Sussex BN7 1XU, England
Distributed in Australia by NewSouth Books
45 Beach Street, Coogee, NSW 2034, Australia

For information about custom editions, special sales, and premium and corporate purchases, please
contact Sterling Special Sales at 800-805-5489 or specialsales@sterlingpublishing.com.

Manufactured in China

Lot #:
2 4 6 8 10 9 7 5 3 1
05/18

sterlingpublishing.com

Interior design by Kevin Ullrich
The artwork for this book was created digitally.

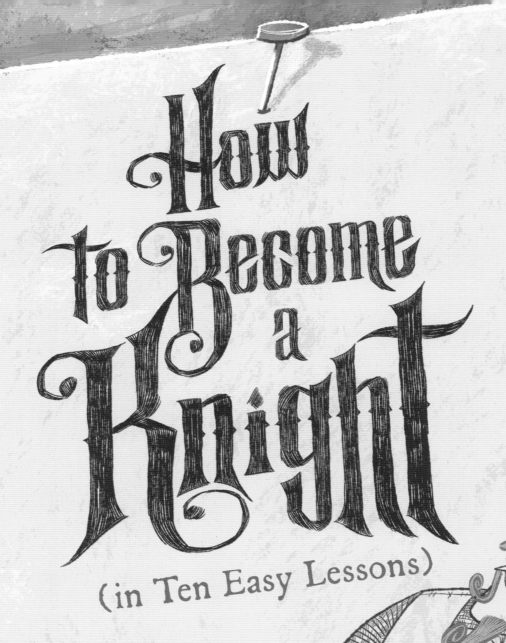

How to Become a Knight

(in Ten Easy Lessons)

by Todd Tarpley

illustrated by Jenn Harney

KNIGHT LESSONS, apply at castle

KNIGHT LESSONS, apply at castle

KNIGHT LESSONS, apply at castle

KNIGHT LESSONS, apply at castle

KNIGHT LESSONS, apply at castle

KNIGHT LESSONS, apply at castle

STERLING CHILDREN'S BOOKS

New York

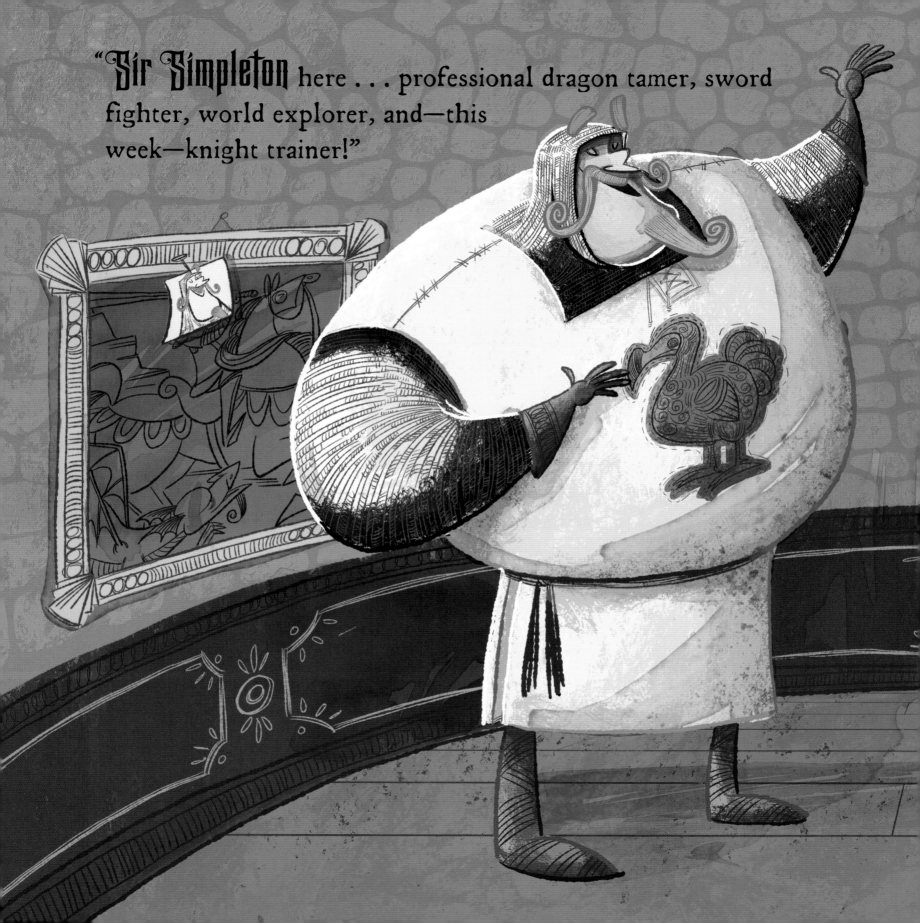

"**Sir Simpleton** here . . . professional dragon tamer, sword fighter, world explorer, and—this week—knight trainer!"

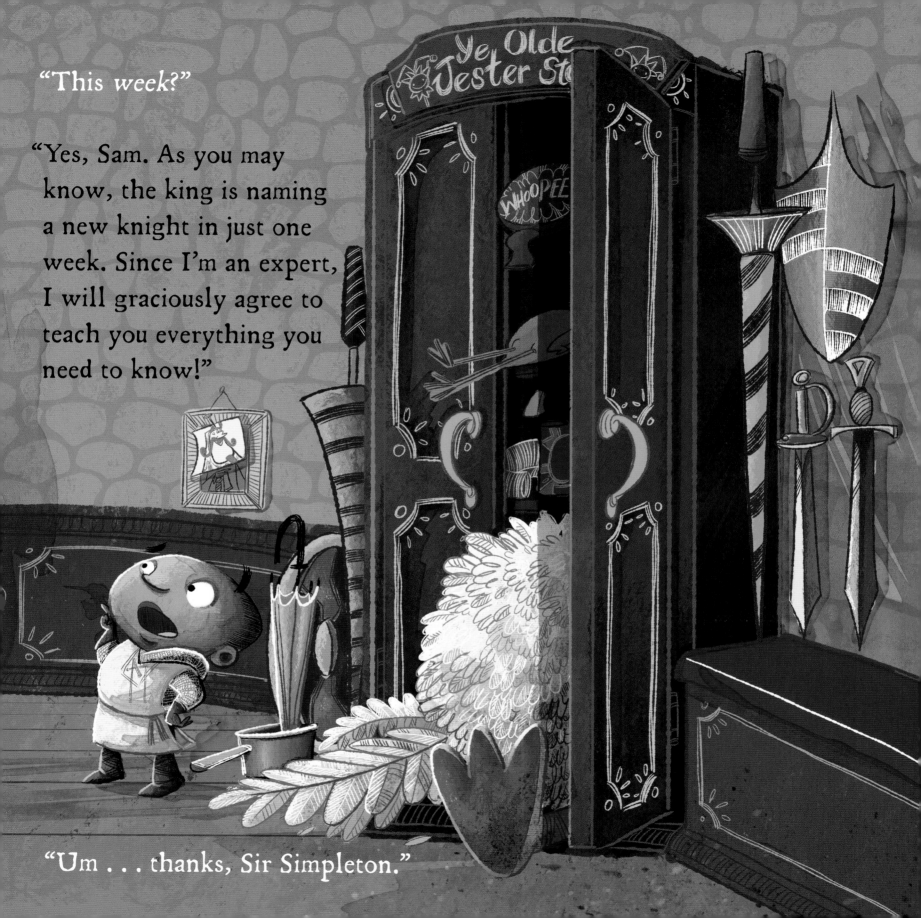

"This *week*?"

"Yes, Sam. As you may know, the king is naming a new knight in just one week. Since I'm an expert, I will graciously agree to teach you everything you need to know!"

"Um . . . thanks, Sir Simpleton."

"Lesson One: Get a bright, shiny suit of armor!
Then no one will be able to poke you with their sword."

"Er . . . Sir Simpleton . . . that doesn't look very bright or shiny.
Are you sure it's really a suit of armor?"

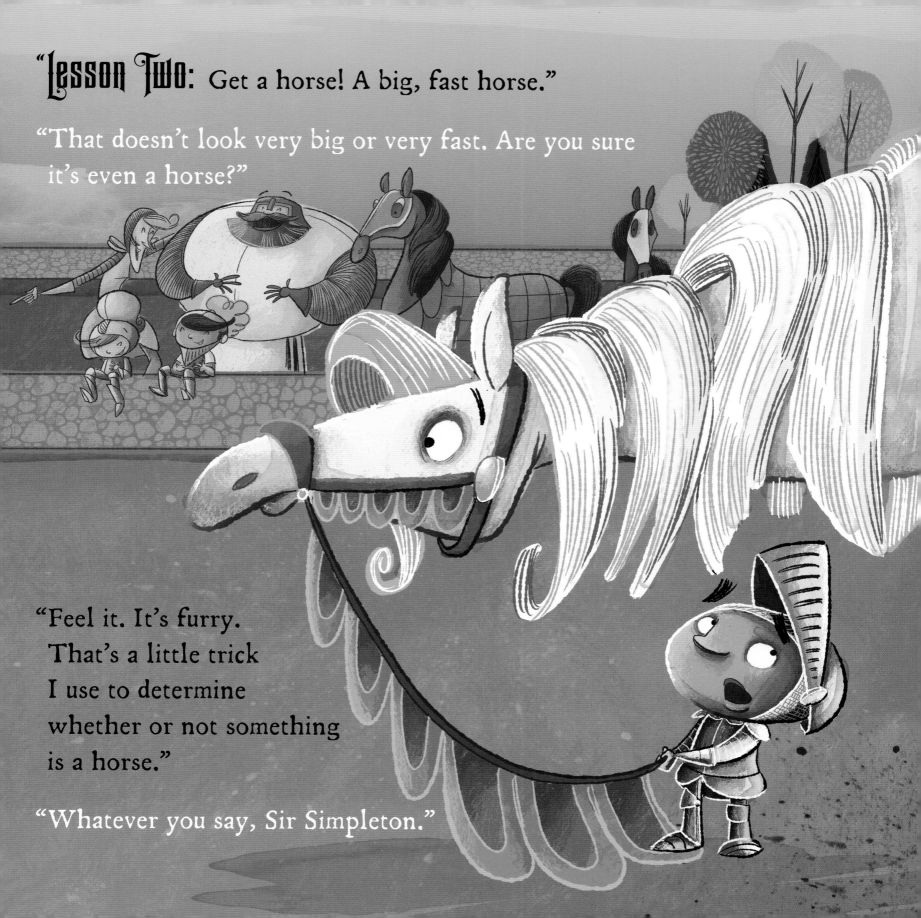

"Lesson Two: Get a horse! A big, fast horse."

"That doesn't look very big or very fast. Are you sure it's even a horse?"

"Feel it. It's furry. That's a little trick I use to determine whether or not something is a horse."

"Whatever you say, Sir Simpleton."

"**Lesson Three:** Defeat a big, scary dragon. This will prove that you are brave."

"That's not a dragon!"

"Focus, Sam. We only have a few more days to go!"

"**Lesson Four:** Rescue a beautiful princess! The princess is the king's daughter, and the king can make you a knight."

"Sir Simpleton?"

"Let me guess. You're going to say this is not a princess. Right?"

"No. I'm going to tell you that your feathers are on fire."

"**Lesson Five:** Be very, very nice to the king! Laugh at all of his jokes and tell him how funny he is."

"That's not the king! That's the court jester!"

"Shhhh! Don't upset him or you'll never become a knight."

Lesson Six: Make friends with other knights! If they like you, they will tell the king to make you a knight."

"Um, Sir Simpleton?"

"I already know what you're going to say, Sam."

"You do?"

"Yes. You are going to thank me for being the world's greatest expert on so many things. And you are welcome."

"Whatever you say, Sir Simpleton."

"Lesson Seven: Seek help from wizards!
They are powerful and can perform magic."

"Sir Simpleton . . ."

"What now?!"

"I've never heard a wizard go
'NEAHH-EHH-EHH.'"

"He's a wizard or
I'm a complete fool!"

"Today is the day, Sam! You are almost ready!

Lesson Eight: When you enter the castle, hold your head high! You want to look very, very important."

"**Lesson Ten:** When the king makes you a knight, kneel and bow your head."

"I'm sorry, Your Highness.
Could you knight him one more time?
I was distracted by all the noise."

"Congratulations, Sam! My expert advice worked.
Of course, you will probably never be as successful as I am,
but don't give up. Keep trying, and with practice,
you will succeed."

"Exactly, Sir Simpleton."